# PROJECT APOLLO

## THE RACE TO LAND ON THE MOON

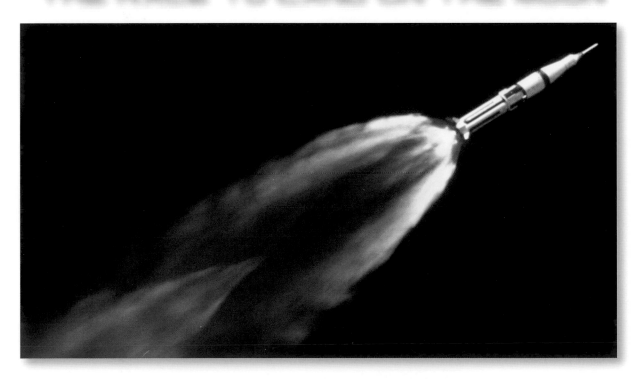

## DAVID JEFFERIS

CRABTREE
PUBLISHING COMPANY
WWW.CRABTREEBOOKS.COM

# INTRODUCTION

The **Apollo** Program, or Project Apollo was a 12-year plan to develop the equipment and skills needed to land humans on the Moon and bring them safely back to Earth. Launched through the National Aeronautics and Space Administration (**NASA**), Apollo included 11 space flights, and six lunar landings. The first crewed lunar landing—of Apollo 11 in 1969—was the high point of the program

 **Crabtree Publishing Company**
www.crabtreebooks.com        1-800-387-7650

Copyright © **2019 CRABTREE PUBLISHING COMPANY**.

**Written and produced for Crabtree Publishing by:**
David Jefferis

**Technical advisor:**
Mat Irvine FBIS (Fellow of the British Interplanetary Society)

**Editors:**
Mat Irvine, Ellen Roger

**Proofreader:**
Melissa Boyce

**Prepress Technicians:**
Mat Irvine, Ken Wright

**Print Coordinator:**
Katherine Berti

**Acknowledgements**
Acknowledgements
We wish to thank all those people who have helped to create this publication and provided images.

Individuals:
Mat Irvine
David Jefferis
Gavin Page
The Design Shop

Organizations:
NASA
Smithsonian National Air and Space Museum
The Observer, London

The right of David Jefferis to be identified as the Author of this work has been asserted by him in accordance with the Copyrights, Designs and Patents Act 1988.

Printed in the U.S.A./042019/CG20190215

**Library and Archives Canada Cataloguing in Publication**

Jefferis, David, author
       Project Apollo : the race to land on the moon / David Jefferis.

(Moon flight atlas)
Includes index.
Issued in print and electronic formats.
ISBN 978-0-7787-5410-7 (hardcover).--
ISBN 978-0-7787-5419-0 (softcover).--
ISBN 978-1-4271-2214-8 (HTML)

       1. Project Apollo (U.S.)--History--Juvenile literature.
2. Project Apollo (U.S.)--History--Sources--Juvenile literature.
3. Space flight to the moon--History--Juvenile literature.
4. Moon--Exploration--History--Juvenile literature.
5. Moon--Maps--Juvenile literature.  I. Title.

TL789.8.U6A5 2019          j629.45'40973          C2018-905619-3
                                                   C2018-905620-7

**Library of Congress Cataloging-in-Publication Data**

Names: Jefferis, David, author.
Title: Project Apollo : the race to land on the Moon / David Jefferis.
Description: New York, New York : Crabtree Publishing Company,
     [2019] |  Series: Moon flight atlas | Includes index.
Identifiers: LCCN 2018060553 (print) | LCCN 2019000504 (ebook) |
     ISBN  9781427122148 (Electronic) |
     ISBN 9780778754107 (hardcover : alk. paper) |
     ISBN 9780778754190 (pbk. : alk. paper)
Subjects: LCSH: Project Apollo (U.S.)--Juvenile literature. | Apollo 11
     (Spacecraft)--Juvenile literature. | Space flight to the moon--Juvenile
     literature. | Moon--Exploration--Juvenile literature.
Classification: LCC TL789.8.U6 (ebook) |
     LCC TL789.8.U6 A541985 2019 (print)  | DDC 629.45/4/0973--dc23
LC record available at https://lccn.loc.gov/2018060553

# MOON FLIGHT ATLAS

# CONTENTS

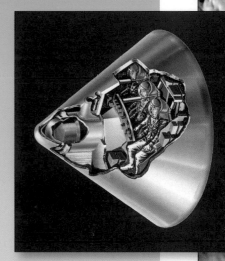

The Apollo program
**4** To the Moon!

The mighty Saturn V
**6** World's biggest rocket

Assembling the Saturn V
**8** The full stack

Command module
**10** Spacecraft for three

Lunar module
**12** Spider in space

Testing Apollo
**14** Tragedy and triumph

Apollo 8 and 10
**16** Circling the Moon

Apollo 11
**18** Target: the Sea of Tranquility

Tranquility base
**20** "One small step"

Return to earth
**22** Safe splashdown

Moon flight facts
**24** Flight path to the surface

**26** Inside story

**28** Timeline

**30** Glossary/Webfinder

**32** Index/About the author

# THE APOLLO PROGRAM
# TO THE MOON!

In 1962, President John F. Kennedy delivered his famous "We choose to go to the Moon" speech. It set the United States on the path of dedicated space exploration that would result in the lunar landing in 1969.

↑ **President Kennedy (*left arrow*) inspects the Mercury spacecraft that John Glenn (*right arrow*) flew into orbit on February 20, 1962.**

**???** **Why did President Kennedy make his speech?**
In an earlier message to Congress on May 25, 1961, President Kennedy said the battle between freedom and **tyranny** in the world would be won when America took a leading role in space achievement. He was referring to the sense of wonder people felt when, in 1957, the **Soviet Union** (U.S.S.R.) launched the first artificial **satellite**, **Sputnik** 1.

This act led to a competition for dominance in space between the U.S. and the U.S.S.R. It was called the Space Race. Kennedy's focus in his message to Congress and his later "We choose to go to the Moon" speech was to land a man on the Moon before the Soviet Union. Project Apollo was the space program that would make it happen.

**???** **What was Apollo?**
This was the name for the entire U.S. Moon program. The Apollo spacecraft (*right*) was designed to carry three astronauts. It followed the smaller single-seat Mercury, and the two-seat Gemini. They all shared a capsule, or small container design.

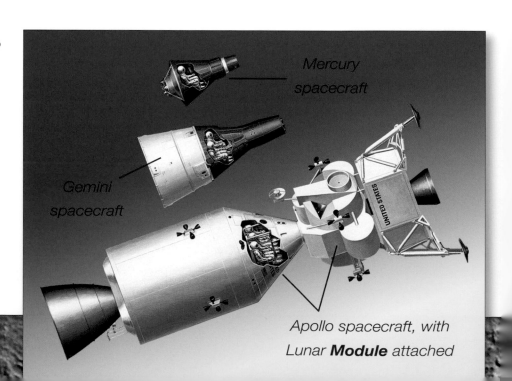

*Mercury spacecraft*

*Gemini spacecraft*

*Apollo spacecraft, with Lunar **Module** attached*

## ??? What was the Saturn V rocket?

This was the big launch rocket that carried Apollo spacecraft and crew into space. Once in space, astronauts would fly to the Moon, which circles, or **orbits**, Earth about 238,000 miles (385,000 km) away.

→ **Wernher von Braun stands near the base of the massive Saturn V rocket. The picture shows four of the five main engines.**

The person who led the design of the Saturn V was Wernher von Braun (*right*). He was a German rocket scientist who had gone to the United States when **World War II** came to an end.

*The Earth and Moon shown to scale*

←↓ **Astronaut John Glenn's Mercury 6 orbit of Earth in 1962 reached 162 miles (261 km) into space. The Moon is about 1,500 times further away. Apollo astronauts faced an enormous challenge in their quest to reach and land on the Moon.**

Earth

*Curving path taken by Apollo spacecraft to and from the Moon*

Moon

# WORLD'S BIGGEST ROCKET

*Escape tower*

*Command Module*

*Service Module*

*Lunar Module housing*

*Third stage*

*Second stage*

*First stage*

**The Saturn V rocket was the core of the Apollo program. Its power made flight to the Moon possible.**

### ??? How big was the Saturn V?

The Saturn V was the tallest rocket ever made. When fully assembled, it towered 363 feet (111 m) high. Fueled up for takeoff, the Saturn V weighed about 3,300 tons (3,000 metric tons). It was heavier than six fully loaded Boeing 747 jumbo jets, each carrying 400 passengers and crew. In all, 13 successful Saturn V flights were made.

### ??? What was the VAB?

VAB stands for the Vehicle Assembly Building (*above*), at Cape Canaveral, Florida. It was an enormous building made to hold all the sections of a Saturn V. At over 525 feet (160 m) high, a complete Saturn rocket could be built in it. The VAB is fully air-conditioned and has the highest bay doors in the world at 456 feet (139 m). They take 45 minutes to open.

### ??? What were the Saturn V's main engines?

Five Rocketdyne F-1 engines were clustered at the base of the Saturn V, the outer four able to swivel for steering. Each F-1 measured 12.2 feet (3.7 m) across. Five were needed to power the rocket to a height of 42 miles (68 km).

"This thing is a pencil as it goes up and it has to be balanced very precisely. And the **gimbaling of the motors, you feel in the seat of your pants...**"

*Michael Collins, Command Module pilot, Apollo 11. He is describing the first moments of lift-off, as the four outer main engines swivel back and forth to keep the Saturn V upright.*

*F-1 engines in the base of the Saturn V*

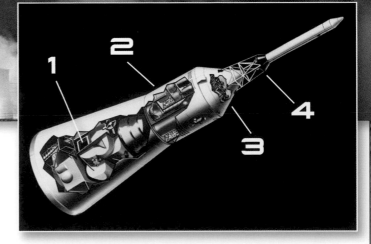

### ??? What fuel did the Saturn V main engines burn?

The five F-1 engines burned a mixture of RP-1 (a type of kerosene) and liquid oxygen. They provided about 3,700 tons (3,400 metric tons) of thrust, propelling the Saturn to a speed of 6,160 miles per hour (9,920 kph).

⬆ On top of the Saturn V were the **Lunar Module (1), Service Module (2), Command Module (3)** and **Launch Escape System (4).**

# THE FULL STACK

The various parts of the Saturn V were assembled in a vertical stack. When this was completed, the huge rocket was ready to be taken from the VAB to the launchpad.

### ??? Where was the Saturn V built and assembled?

The parts for each Saturn V were built by various **aerospace contractors**, including Boeing, Douglas, and North American Aviation. IBM supplied many of the computer components. When finished, they were all delivered to the VAB for final assembly, or "stacking."

The Saturn V was the biggest of three Saturn-family rockets, the 1, 1B, and V. They were all designed by teams led by Wernher von Braun.

### ??? What were the Saturn V's main parts?

These were the three rocket stages. The S-IC first stage was used for lift-off, and was dropped into the sea when its fuel was used up.

The S-II second stage took over, until it too ran out of fuel—a mixture of liquid oxygen and hydrogen.

The S-IVB third stage went into orbit with the Apollo spacecraft, traveling at just over 17,500 miles per hour (28,000 kph).

← The Lunar Module (LM) was made to land on the Moon. Here, a partly built LM is being checked in the VAB.

"NASA has been one of the most successful public investments in motivating students to do well and achieve all they can achieve." *Neil Armstrong, first human on the Moon, Apollo 11. The whole Apollo program was run by NASA, the U.S. agency created in 1958.*

⬆ The technicians (*arrowed*) give a fair idea of the huge size of the VAB. Here, the Apollo 8 spacecraft is shown being stacked.

**??? How did Saturn stages arrive?**

The first stage was built in Louisiana, and delivered on a barge. The second stage was made in California, and brought by ship. The smaller third stage was also built in California, but could be flown in a large cargo plane.

**??? What were the crawler-transporters?**

They were two huge machines, nicknamed "Hans" and "Franz," that moved on metal tracks, rather than wheels. They carried an entire Apollo stack, at a speed of up to 1 mile per hour (1.6 kph). The route led from the VAB to a launchpad, on a road called the "crawlerway." After the Apollo program ended, the massive machines were used for Space Shuttle launches, from 1981 to 2011.

# COMMAND MODULE
# SPACECRAFT FOR THREE

The Command Module (CM) was designed for three astronauts. The attached Service Module (SM) had a rocket motor, and held supplies needed by the crew.

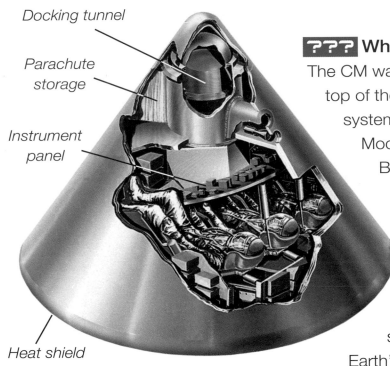

Docking tunnel

Parachute storage

Instrument panel

Heat shield

**??? What was in the Command Module?**

The CM was a kind of base for operations. At the top of the forward compartment were steering systems, a **docking** tunnel to the Lunar Module, and parachutes, stored for landing. Below this was a crew compartment, flight controls, equipment bays, and electronic systems. Under the crew compartment were more steering systems, freshwater tanks, and cables connected to the Service Module. At the base was the heat shield, needed to return safely through Earth's **atmosphere**.

"I am alone now, truly alone, and absolutely isolated from any known life. I am it."
*Michael Collins, Apollo 11, talking about staying in the Command Module while Armstrong and Aldrin were on the Moon's surface*

**??? Was the Command Module a comfortable environment for the crew?**

It was certainly a close fit! The cone-shaped CM was just 12.8 feet (3.9 m) wide, so placing three astronauts and their equipment inside was a major achievement in planning.

Also, missions lasted for eight days or more, so personal hygiene was important. The capsule had no washroom, so astronauts filled sealable bags with liquid waste. For solid matter, they used diaper-like bags, held on with tape. Afterwards, they cleaned up with medical wipes.

## ??? Why was the CM called the "mother ship"?

A mother ship is a base or headquarters of operations. When linked together, the Apollo Command and Service Modules were called the CSM. They formed the mother ship for the Moon mission. The cylindrical SM had a rocket motor and fuel tanks for propulsion, with storage bays for other equipment. This included **fuel cells**, which provided electric power, oxygen, and water. Later Apollo missions had a Scientific Instrument Module (SIM) bay, which carried a number of cameras and other measuring equipment.

→ **The CSM in flight mode. The main engine at the back was used to slow down into lunar orbit. It was fired again to return to Earth.**

↑ **The three crew seats were placed side by side, with the wide, main instrument panel mounted in front.**

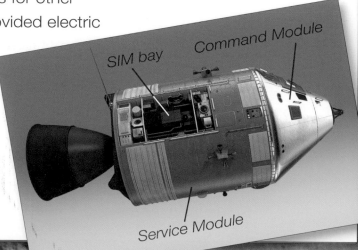

SIM bay

Command Module

Service Module

# LUNAR MODULE
# SPIDER IN SPACE

The Apollo Lunar Module (LM) was the spacecraft built to land on the Moon's surface. It had two main sections, the descent, or downward stage, and the ascent, or upward stage.

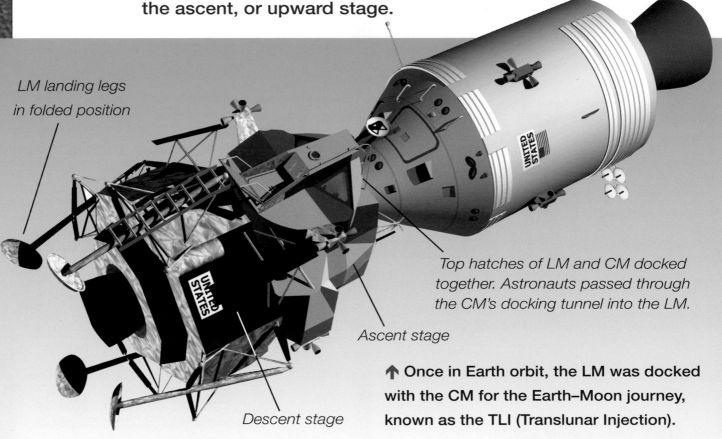

*LM landing legs in folded position*

*Top hatches of LM and CM docked together. Astronauts passed through the CM's docking tunnel into the LM.*

*Ascent stage*

*Descent stage*

**↑ Once in Earth orbit, the LM was docked with the CM for the Earth–Moon journey, known as the TLI (Translunar Injection).**

### ??? Why did the LM's legs fold up?

The LM's legs were designed so the whole craft could be loaded tightly into the Saturn V rocket. In space, the legs spread out to the lunar-landing position. The LM was made to work only in space or on the airless Moon. Saving weight was important, so there were no seats, and the crew stood during flight. They also had no beds to sleep on and used hammocks instead.

"You don't select astronauts who want fame and fortune. You select them because they're the best test pilots in the world..." *Alan Shepard, Mercury astronaut and commander, Apollo 14*

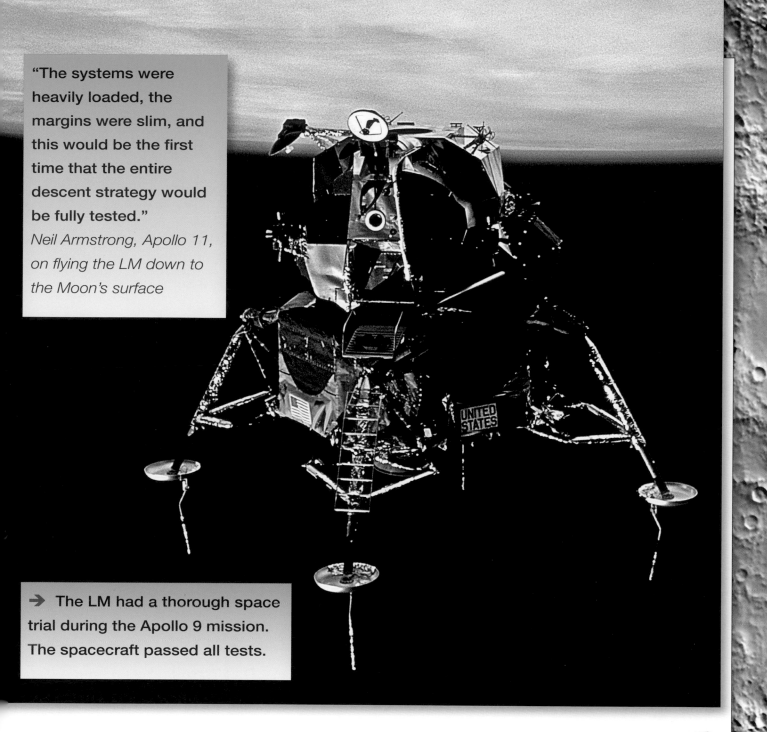

→ The LM had a thorough space trial during the Apollo 9 mission. The spacecraft passed all tests.

### ??? Why were long probes attached to the legs?

Contact probes were used to signal the LM astronauts the moment they touched the Moon.

The Apollo 9 LM (*above*) was tested in Earth orbit with four probes, but the one under the ladder was later removed in case it punctured a space suit after landing.

→ Astronauts used the Lunar Landing Research Vehicle (LLRV) for landing practice on Earth. The LLRV was difficult to fly. In fact, three crashed. Luckily, no one was killed.

# TESTING APOLLO
# TRAGEDY AND TRIUMPH

A flash fire during training killed the crew of Apollo 1. The CSM was then redesigned for safety.

**??? Why did Apollo 1 catch fire?**
Apollo 1 was designed as the first test flight of the CSM for launch on a Saturn 1B (*right*), a smaller version of the Saturn V rocket. During a practice session on January 27, 1967, a fire broke out in the CM. Deadly smoke and carbon monoxide gas filled the small space. By the time the hatch could be opened, the astronauts inside—Gus Grissom, Ed White, and Roger Chaffee—were dead.

➜ The Saturn 1B launched several missions, including Apollo 7 in 1968.

↑ The burned hulk of the Apollo 1 Command Module.

**??? When was a new Command Module ready?**
The Apollo 1 fire brought any further testing of the Command Module to a sudden halt. It had to be completely redesigned, with changes that included a quick-release hatch. The existing hatch had trapped the astronauts inside until it was too late to escape. Adjustments were made to the CM air supply to reduce the chances of a flash fire in future. Flammable materials were also removed or replaced as much as possible.

↑ Cameras on an uncrewed test flight captured this moment as an empty stage is left behind. Seen here is an interstage, a section that joins two stages together.

→ Apollo missions all started from Cape Canaveral, in the VAB (*1*). A stacked Saturn rocket was taken along the crawlerway (*2*), to one of two launchpads (*3*, *4*) next to the Atlantic Ocean.

## ??? What happened to future Apollo flights?

Changes to the Command Module were made, though a new design was not ready for 21 months. Astronauts finally returned to space in October 1968, with Apollo 7. It orbited Earth for 11 days. This successful orbit cleared the way for the next big step—an Apollo flight around the Moon and back.

→ The first TV show from space was made aboard Apollo 7.

KEEP THOSE CARDS AND LETTERS COMING IN FOLKS

# CIRCLING THE MOON

Apollo 8 and 10 were test flights to test systems for a future lunar landing. Crews flew around the Moon and became the first humans to see its far, or dark, side.

⬆ The Apollo 8 crew, from left: James Lovell, William Anders, and Frank Borman.

### ??? What was special about the Apollo 8 mission?

Launched on December 21, 1968, Apollo 8 was the first crewed mission to leave Earth orbit. Frank Borman, James Lovell, and William Anders made the three-day voyage to the Moon and circled it 10 times.

"The vast loneliness up here at the moon is awe-inspiring, and it makes you realize what you have back there on Earth. The Earth from here is a grand oasis in the big vastness of space."
*James Lovell, Apollo 8 CM pilot, on looking back at our world hanging in space*

### ??? What did the mission achieve?

The Apollo 8 crew were the first to directly see the Moon's far side. This side always faces away, and cannot be seen from Earth. Apollo 8's greatest achievement though, was proving that humans could survive the journey to the Moon. It paved the way for future missions, including Apollo 9, which tested the Lunar Module in Earth orbit.

⬆ Earthrise is the name of a famous photo of Earth taken by Apollo 8 astronaut William Anders while in lunar orbit.

← Eugene Cernan suits up for Apollo 10, launched on May 18, 1969.

→ Necho crater on the far side of the Moon, as seen from Apollo 10. It is 19 miles (30 km) wide.

## ??? What was the aim of the Apollo 10 mission?

Apollo 10 was the full dress rehearsal for a Moon landing—except for the landing itself. So the flight went into orbit around the Moon, just like Apollo 8. Then astronauts Thomas Stafford and Eugene Cernan flew the LM to within 8.4 miles (13.5 km) of the surface. They nearly didn't come back though, as the spacecraft went briefly out of control. It went into a rolling motion, but they managed to steady the LM just in time.

"The [LM] fuel tanks weren't full. So had we literally tried to land on the Moon, we couldn't have gotten off." *Eugene Cernan, Apollo 10, on how mission planners made sure there was no attempt to make an "unofficial" landing before Apollo 11*

A U.S. Navy helicopter hovers over the Apollo 10 CM shortly after **splashdown**

## ??? What was the Apollo 10 "space music"?

While passing over the lunar far side, the crew heard an odd whistling noise for about an hour. NASA believes it was a form of radio interference between the Command and Lunar Modules. The unusual "music" was never heard again, although some people who believe in UFOs think it was an alien message. There is no proof of this.

# TARGET: THE SEA OF TRANQUILITY

Apollo 8, 9, and 10 were all successful. Now it was time to try for the main mission—to orbit the Moon, then fly down and land safely on its surface.

**??? Why was the Sea of Tranquility chosen for the landing?**
Previous Apollo missions, as well as space probes, had mapped the best places for landing. These included a reasonably flat area that would be in sunlight for the whole time that astronauts were on the surface.

*Metal connector ring for helmet*

*Soft skullcap held earphones and microphone*

**??? How was the Apollo 11 crew chosen?**
The idea was that any crew member could fly any mission, in case mission objectives changed, or an astronaut got sick. So there was always a backup crew ready, just in case. In fact, Neil Armstrong (*left*) and Buzz Aldrin had been backups for Apollo 9. For Apollo 11, Neil was chosen because he was calm under pressure. He had been a test pilot earlier in his career.

← Neil Armstrong, waiting before the launch. He has yet to put on his clear plastic "fishbowl" helmet.

> "A typical smart phone has more computing power than Apollo 11 when it landed a man on the Moon."
>
> *Nancy Gibbs, journalist*

← The full-stack Apollo 11 Saturn V is taken slowly along the crawlerway leading to the launchpad.

### ??? What would have happened if Apollo 11 hadn't landed?

Apollo 11 was the first landing attempt, so success was uncertain. President Kennedy had promised to land "before this decade is out." This left just enough time in 1969 for two more Apollo attempts, if needed.

If an LM was stranded on the Moon, then-President Richard Nixon had a speech prepared to mark such a tragedy. Luckily, he never had to give that speech.

### ??? How long did the flight take?

Apollo 11 left the launchpad on July 16, 1969. From there to entering orbit around the Moon, the flight took 75 hours and 56 minutes. The next step was to power up the LM and go for a landing.

→ Helmets on, Buzz Aldrin (*1*), Michael Collins (*2*), and Neil Armstrong (*3*) walk to their waiting spacecraft.

# "ONE SMALL STEP"

Neil Armstrong and Buzz Aldrin went down in the history books when they landed the Lunar Module Eagle on the Sea of Tranquility, on July 20, 1969.

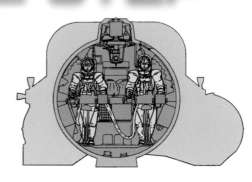

### ??? What was the LM like to fly?

It was tricky. They had trained with the Lunar Landing Training Vehicle (LLTV) on Earth, but in the Eagle they missed their target on the Moon. They neared the landing zone, only to find it was littered with boulders, any of which could tip them over. Armstrong flew to a safe spot and landed with just 30 seconds of fuel remaining!

↑ The LM had no seats. Instead, the crew stood at the controls.

### ??? When did they step on the surface?

After the landing, the two astronauts had a rest period lasting six hours. Then they checked their space suits, and opened the LM's front hatch.

Armstrong crawled onto the porch, went down the ladder, and took the first steps on the Moon. Nineteen minutes later, Buzz Aldrin joined him.

↑ The LM (*left*) had two windows for the crew to see out. Here, Buzz Aldrin makes progress with placing equipment.

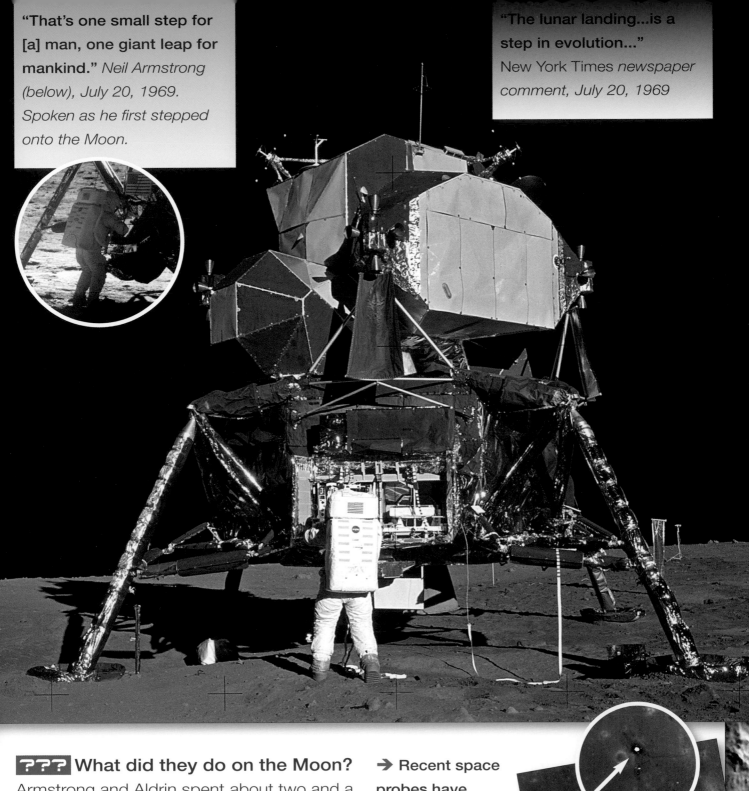

**???** **What did they do on the Moon?**

Armstrong and Aldrin spent about two and a quarter hours walking on the Moon. They set up science instruments, one of which is still in working order. They also collected samples of Moon rocks—47.5 pounds (21.5 kg) in all—for scientists waiting on Earth.

→ **Recent space probes have spotted the Apollo 11 landing site. The LM descent stage (*arrowed*) is visible in this image.**

Apollo 11 Site

200 meters

# RETURN TO EARTH
# SAFE SPLASHDOWN

The voyage home was the last hurdle remaining for a successful Apollo 11 mission. First, they had to leave the Moon and dock with the Command Module in orbit above.

### ??? How long were Armstrong and Aldrin on the surface?

After a stay on the Moon lasting 21.5 hours, Armstrong and Aldrin fired the LM ascent-stage engine to return to the Command Module. There, they would meet Michael Collins, who was waiting for them in the CM.

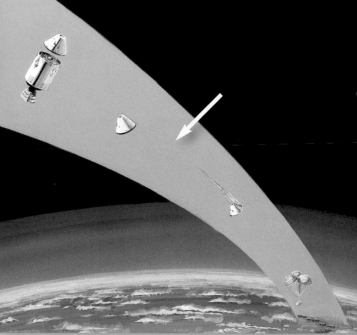

### ??? How did they return to the Command Module?

The picture above was taken by Collins as the Eagle approached the CM Columbia. The two craft docked, and the three astronauts were together again. The Eagle was left behind, and they used the CSM engine to blast free of Moon orbit and begin the three-day journey back to Earth.

↑ The CM had to enter the Earth's atmosphere at a special angle, called the **entry corridor** (*arrowed*). Too high, and the CM would skip off into space. Too low, and it would burn up and crash.

### ??? Where did they land?

Before entry into Earth's atmosphere, the Service Module was detached and left to burn up. Columbia made a perfect entry (*left*) and splashed down in the Pacific Ocean. The mission lasted more than eight days.

"We would like to give special thanks to all those Americans who built the spacecraft; who did the construction, design, the tests, and put their hearts and all their abilities into those craft." *Neil Armstrong, Apollo 11, July 23, 1969*

### ??? What happened next?

Project Apollo was a complete success. Apollo 11 fulfilled the aims of John F. Kennedy in his 1961 and 1962 speeches. After Armstrong and Aldrin's triumph came five more landings. The last three—Apollo 15, 16, and 17— took a lunar rover electric car to explore further from their landing sites.

Was Apollo worth the effort? Absolutely. It was a fantastic investment in science research and technology, much of which we use today.

↑ Air-filled flotation bags kept the capsule afloat after splashdown.

# FLIGHT PATH TO THE SURFACE

Armstrong and Aldrin flew the Eagle down a precise landing path to the Moon's surface. They used automated controls to start their descent. Then, Armstrong took over and landed manually.

**???** **Were there any landing problems?**

There was an alarm signal at one point, but Mission Control believed all was well, saying "...we're GO on that alarm." At 40 feet (12 m) above the surface, Aldrin noted that the engine exhaust was "...kicking up some dust." Just moments later, Aldrin announced "Contact light. Okay. Engine stop." They were on the surface. The Eagle had landed.

← Apollo planners picked the Sea of Tranquility for the first landing attempt.

→ This NASA chart shows the flight path for Apollo 11, the LM approaching from the right (*1*). The LM descent engine started braking for landing (*2*). Speed and height were gradually reduced until the Eagle touched down in the landing zone (*3*).

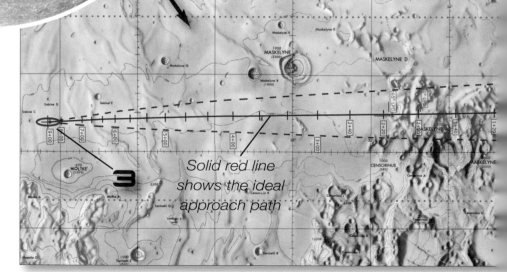

*Solid red line shows the ideal approach path*

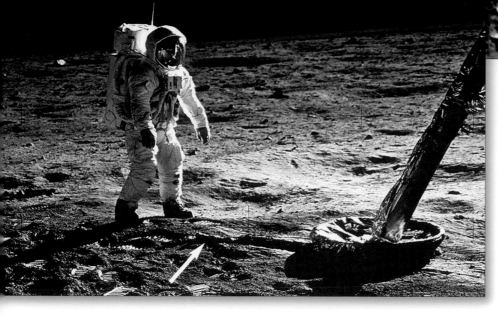

HERE MEN FROM THE PLANET EARTH FIRST SET FOOT UPON THE MOON JULY 1969, A. D.
WE CAME IN PEACE FOR ALL MANKIND

MICHAEL COLLINS
ASTRONAUT

EDWIN E. ALDRIN, JR.
ASTRONAUT

NEIL A. ARMSTRONG
ASTRONAUT

RICHARD NIXON
PRESIDENT, UNITED STATES OF AMERICA

↑ Buzz Aldrin, standing by the LM. One of the landing probes (*arrowed*) lies flat on the soil by his feet. Armstrong carried the camera and took almost all the photographs.

↑ This metal plaque was placed on an LM landing leg. It is still on the Moon.

### ??? Was leaving the Moon free of problems?

Not quite. A last-minute obstacle occurred when an electrical switch was broken.

Luckily, inserting a pen in the gap was enough to fix the problem. It allowed the LM to take off and meet the CSM—and Michael Collins.

"The surface of the moon is like nothing here on Earth! It's totally lacking any evidence of life. It has lots of fine, talcum-powderlike dust mixed with a complete variety of pebbles, rocks, and boulders...The dust is a very fine, overall dark gray. And with no air molecules to separate the dust, it clings together like cement."
*Buzz Aldrin, Apollo 11, second human to walk on the Moon. Aldrin also coined the words "magnificent desolation" to describe how he felt about the scenery of the Moon.*

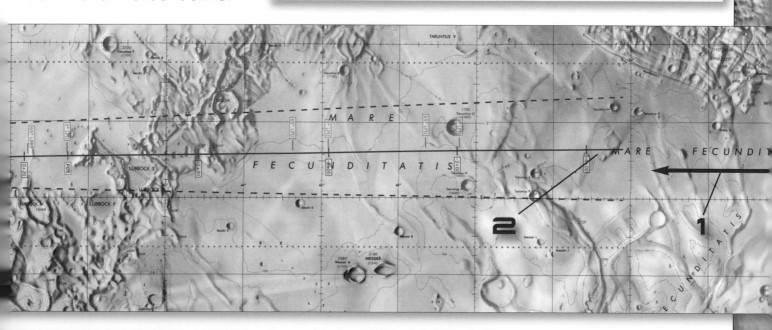

# INSIDE STORY

What went on inside the huge 3,300-ton (3,000 metric ton) Apollo-Saturn V launch rocket?

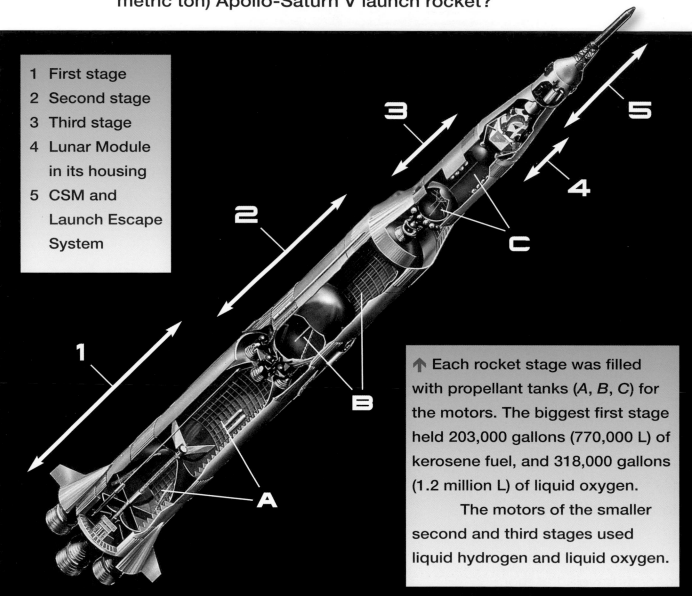

1  First stage
2  Second stage
3  Third stage
4  Lunar Module in its housing
5  CSM and Launch Escape System

↑ Each rocket stage was filled with propellant tanks (A, B, C) for the motors. The biggest first stage held 203,000 gallons (770,000 L) of kerosene fuel, and 318,000 gallons (1.2 million L) of liquid oxygen.

The motors of the smaller second and third stages used liquid hydrogen and liquid oxygen.

## ??? How powerful was the Saturn V?

The Saturn V rocket was made of more than 3 million parts. When loaded with propellants, or the fuels that gave it thrust power, the three-stage rocket weighed nearly 3,300 tons (3,000 metric tons). And at full thrust, the five F-1 first-stage engines produced enough energy to light up a large city for hours.

← Here, the Saturn second stage is lifted by crane onto a test stand. Once the stage was in position, technicians could measure the performance of the five J-2 engines.

## ??? What did the Saturn V's three stages do?

The first stage fired for about 2.5 minutes, to a height of about 38 miles (61 km). Then, with the fuel used up, the stage separated. It dropped into the ocean far below. The second stage took over, firing for six minutes, to a height of 115 miles (185 km), before it also fell away.

The third stage had two jobs. First, it placed the CSM and LM into Earth orbit. Then, after checks had been made, the rocket motor fired again. This was called the Translunar Injection. With it, the Apollo spacecraft traveled at more than 24,500 miles per hour (39,430 kph).

→ While being put together, Apollo 11's newly built modules were wrapped in plastic sheets for protection.

# TIMELINE

The beginning of the Space Race, from the first orbits to the lunar landing and the end of the Apollo missions.

### 1958–1963 Project Mercury

The single-seat Mercury program was established to get an American in space as quickly as possible. This was the start of the Space Race.

1961  On May 5,  Alan Shepard becomes the first American in space, on board the Mercury spacecraft Freedom 7.
 Five more Mercury missions follow, including the first orbital flight in 1962, flown by John Glenn.

### 1962–1966 Project Gemini

The next program from Mercury, designed to further space travel for the Apollo Moon program.

1965–1966  Many space achievements are made using the two-seat Gemini spacecraft, the first crewed mission being flown by Virgil "Gus" Grissom and John Young, who fly for three orbits around Earth.
 Eleven further Gemini missions follow, the last in November 1966. Their achievements make way for the Apollo flights to come.

← Powerful Saturn V rockets made the Apollo program possible. Here, Apollo 4 takes off in November 1967. This was an uncrewed mission, the first test flight of the Saturn V.

## 1961–1972 Project Apollo

**1964–1968** Sixteen Apollo uncrewed flights are flown, testing various types of rockets and different equipment.

**1967** Apollo 1 fire in January kills all three crew members while they are on the launchpad.

**1968** Apollo 7 first crewed flight in October, using the redesigned Command Module.

**1968** The first humans leave Earth orbit in Apollo 8. The flight is not a landing mission. Instead, they orbit the Moon 10 times, then return to Earth.

**1969** The Apollo 9 flight in March tests all hardware, including the Lunar Module. Astronauts check the system in Earth orbit for 10 days, undocking and then redocking the LM with the Command Module.

**1969** Apollo 10 is a second round-the-Moon mission, a dress rehearsal for the actual landing attempt.

**1969** On July 20, astronauts Neil Armstrong and Buzz Aldrin become the first humans on the Moon on the Apollo 11 mission.

**1969–1972** Apollo 11 is followed by the successful landings of Apollo 12, 14, 15, 16, and 17.
  The Apollo 13 mission suffers a Service Module explosion on the way to the Moon. The crew survives by using the LM

↑ A huge welcome parade was held in New York for returning Apollo crews. Here are (*arrowed from left*) **Buzz Aldrin, Michael Collins,** and **Neil Armstrong,** from Apollo 11.

as a space lifeboat, and return safely home to Earth.

**1972** By the time of the last Apollo landing in 1972, total funding for the program had reached about $20 billion. That's a lot of money, but the weekly cost to each American was only about the same as buying a box of breakfast cereal.

"He eats, lives, and breathes space, and he's got a whole bunch of ideas, usually pretty good ideas, about our future. He's mister space, space, space."
*Michael Collins, Apollo 11, talking about Buzz Aldrin, his crewmate on that mission*

# GLOSSARY

**Apollo** The U.S. Moon-landing program, named after the Greek and Roman gods of light and beauty

**aerospace contractors** Private companies that build space technology such as rockets and landers

**atmosphere** The envelope of gases surrounding Earth or another planet

**docking** Procedure in which two spacecraft approach each other, then link together.

**entry corridor** A safe path that a spacecraft has to take when entering Earth's atmosphere

**fuel cell** Equipment that generates electricity by combining hydrogen and oxygen, with pure water as waste

**gimbal** Part of a Saturn V rocket motor that allowed it to tilt slightly to keep the whole vehicle steady during launch

**Launch Escape System (LES)** A rocket above the Command Module at launch that carries it to safety in the event of a launch failure

**module** Section of a spacecraft that links with another. The Apollo system consisted of a number of such modules:

　　**CM** Command Module

　　**SM** Service Module

　　**LM** Lunar Module

When linked together, the CM and SM were called the CSM.

**NASA** National Aeronautics and Space Administration, the U.S. space agency

**orbit** The curving path that one space object takes around another

**satellite** A space object that orbits a larger one

**Soviet Union** A group of 15 states, including Russia, that existed from 1922

← View of the Apollo 11 CSM, in orbit around the Moon with Michael Collins aboard.

↑ The Little Joe II rocket tested the Launch Escape System in case of a launch failure. In fact, all Saturn V launches were successful.

to 1991. Also known as the Union of Soviet Socialist Republics (U.S.S.R.).

**splashdown** Final part of an Apollo mission when the Apollo CM parachuted into the sea. The floating CM and astronauts were then taken to a nearby ship.

**Sputnik** Word used for several early Soviet satellites. It means "fellow traveller" in Russian.

**stage** Part of a rocket, usually one of several used to boost a rocket into space and then left behind when empty of fuel

**tyranny** Cruel or oppressive rule by a ruler of government

**World War II** A global war from 1939 to 1945 involving the Allies, including Britain, the U.S., and Canada, against the Axis powers, including Germany, Japan, and Italy

# WEBFINDER

There is plenty of Internet information on the Apollo missions, and even more on space exploration in general. Try these sites to start with, then you can go off on your own online explorations.

**www.buzzaldrin.com**
Buzz Aldrin stepped onto the Moon after Neil Armstrong, but he is a leader on the Internet. Here is his fascinating personal website.

**www.canada.ca/en/space-agency**
Canada's space industry has a long history, and its robotic equipment works hard in orbit. Start here to find the whole story.

**www.firstmenonthemoon.com**
A fascinating site, with the view from the Apollo 11 LM matched to the radio chat between astronauts and Mission Control. It sounds like the landing could have happened just yesterday!

**www.nasa.gov**
The gold standard for space research, including Apollo, Mercury, Gemini, and other programs. Just use the online search box to find out more.

**www.spacex.com**
Site of this 21st-century space pioneer, SpaceX has Moon missions already planned for the near future. Flights are often broadcast live.

"As a former Apollo astronaut, I think it's safe to say that SpaceX and the other commercial developers embody the 21st century version of the Apollo frontier spirit."
*Russell "Rusty" Schweickart, Apollo 9 Lunar Module pilot*

# INDEX

aerospace companies
  Boeing 6, 8
  Douglas 8
  IBM 8
  North American
    Aviation 8
  SpaceX 31
Apollo (history of
  missions) 31
astronauts
  Aldrin, Edwin "Buzz"
    18, 19, 20, 21, 22,
    23, 25, 29, 31
  Anders, William 16
  Armstrong, Neil 9, 10,
    18, 19, 20, 21, 22,
    23, 24, 25, 29
  Borman, Frank 16
  Cernan, Eugene 17
  Chaffee, Roger 14
  Collins, Michael 7, 10,
    19, 22, 25, 29, 30
  Duke, Charlie 27
  Glenn, John 4, 5, 28
  Grissom, Gus 14, 28
  Lovell, James 16
  Schweickart, Russell
    31
  Shepard, Alan 12, 28
  White, Ed 14
  Young, John 28
atmosphere 10, 22, 23,
  30

contact light, probe 13,
  24
cost (of Apollo program)
  29

crawler-transporter 9

docking (maneuver) 10,
  12, 30

entry corridor 22, 30

fire (in Apollo 1) 14
flotation bags 23
Franz, Hans (see crawler-
  transporter)
fuel cells 11, 30

gimbal 7, 30

kerosene (fuel) 7, 26

LES (Launch Escape
  System) 7, 26, 30, 31
liquid hydrogen 8, 26
liquid oxygen 7, 8, 26
LLRV (Lunar Landing
  Research Vehicle) 13
lunar rover 23

Mission Control 24, 27
Moon
  far side 16, 17
  Necho crater 17
  plaque 25
  rocks 21
  Sea of Tranquility 18,
    20, 24, 27

NASA 2, 9, 18, 24
New York Times 21

orbit 4, 8, 11, 12, 13, 16,
  18, 19, 20, 22, 27, 29,
  30, 31

people
  Braun, Wernher von 5,
    8
  Gibbs, Nancy 19
  Kennedy, John F. 4, 5,
    19, 23
  Nixon, Richard 19
  Rees, Martin 15
personal hygiene 10
places (on Earth)
  Atlantic Ocean 15
  California 9
  Cape Canaveral 6, 15
  Louisiana 9
  Pacific Ocean 23
  Soviet Union 4, 31
  United States 4, 5, 31

Rocketdyne F-1 engine
  7, 26

satellites 4, 30, 31
SIM (Scientific Instrument
  Module) 11
space music 17
Space Race 4, 28, 31
spacecraft
  Columbia 22
  Eagle 20, 23, 24
  Freedom 7 28
  Gemini 4, 28
  Mercury 4, 5, 12, 28,
    31
  Space Shuttle 9

Sputnik 4, 31
splashdown 17, 22, 23,
  31
stack 8, 9, 19

TLI (Translunar Injection)
  12, 27
TV show (from Apollo 7)
  15

VAB (Vehicle Assembly
  Building) 6, 8, 9, 15,
  27

World War II 5

# ABOUT THE AUTHOR

David Jefferis has written many information books on science and technology.

His works include a seminal series called World of the Future, as well as more than 40 science books for Crabtree Publishing.

David's merits include winning the London Times Educational Supplement Award, and also Best Science Books of the Year.

At the time of the Apollo landings, he created news graphics for the international media, and has been a keen enthusiast for space flight and high tech ever since.

Follow David online at:
www.davidjefferis.com